The Beginner's Bible®

Super Girls of the Bible

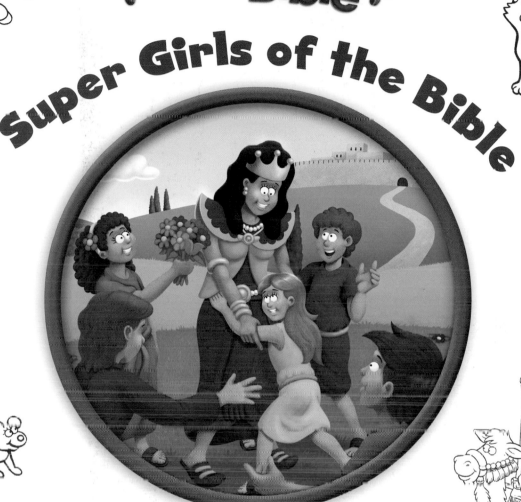

Sticker & Activity Book

ZONDERkidz

Copyright © 2015 by Zonderkidz

Requests for information should be addressed to:
Zonderkidz, 3900 Sparks Drive SE, Grand Rapids, Michigan 49546

Design: Jody Langley

Printed in China

Color in the Bible women.

Martha

Mary

Eve

Super Girls

There are many great women and girls in the Bible. They weren't always perfect. Sometimes they made mistakes. But they loved God, and God used them to do wonderful things.

Esther

Rahab

Anna

Deborah

Deborah Leads the Way

Deborah was a judge. She loved God very much. God gave her a plan to defeat the bad king who ruled over the Israelites.

Find the stickers to finish the pictures.

Circle the words that rhyme with BAD.

DAD

MAD

TREE

DOG

GLAD

FISH

SAD

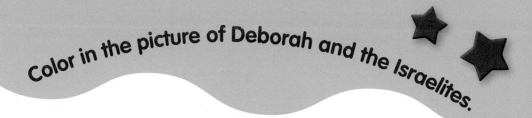

A Mighty Victory

Deborah and a man named Barak took 10,000 soldiers to the top of a hill. When Deborah told them to attack the bad king's army, the Israelites obeyed. They won the battle!

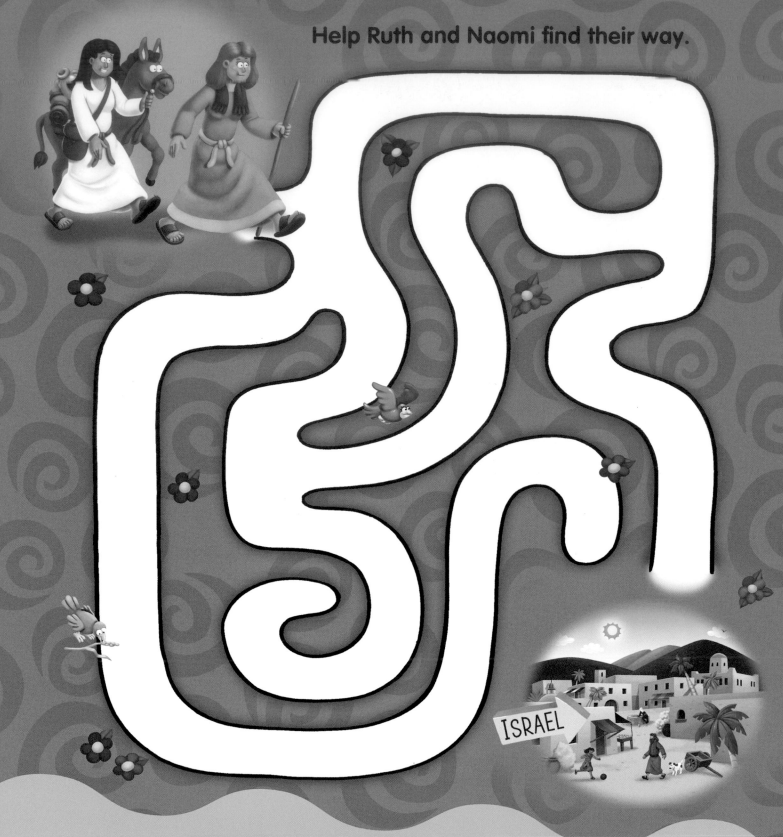

ISRAEL

Ruth and Naomi

Naomi's husband died. She decided to go back to her homeland. Her daughter-in-law Ruth went with her. Help Ruth and Naomi find their way to Israel.

A New Family

Ruth loved Naomi. She took care of her. Every day, Ruth went out into the fields to gather leftover grain for them to eat. Eventually, God blessed Ruth and Naomi with a brand-new family.

Count the bundles of grain.
Circle the number in each group below.

1   (2)   3

2   3   4

1   2   3

3   4   5

Hannah's Prayer

Hannah was a super girl of the Bible. She loved God. She wanted to have a baby, but she wasn't able to have any children.

Draw a line from the mothers to their babies.

Baby Blessing

Hannah prayed to God, "If you give me a baby boy, I will see that he serves you all his life." God heard Hannah's prayer. Soon, Hannah and her husband had a baby boy. They thanked God for their new son.

Use the stickers to fill in the missing puzzle pieces.

Trace and write the word BABY.

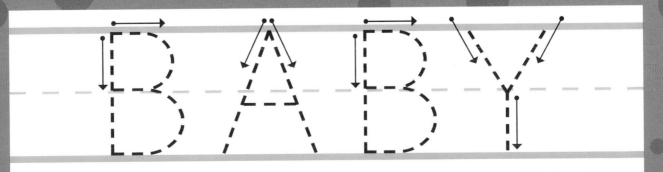

The Brave Queen

Esther was another super girl of the Bible. She was very beautiful. The King of Persia chose her to be his queen.

You are beautiful because God made you. Draw a picture of yourself in the mirror.

A Risky Plan

Esther saved her people from a bad man named Haman.
She told the king about Haman's plan to get rid of the
Jewish people. The Jewish people were so happy!

Use the
stickers to
finish the
pictures.

Then What Happened?

Mary was the mother of Jesus. An angel appeared and told her she was going to have a baby. She said, "I love God. I will do what he has chosen me to do."

Mary was with Jesus as he grew up.

Look at the pictures. Write the number 1 below what happened first. Write the number 2 below what happened second. Write the number 3 below what happened third. Write the number 4 below what happened last.

Mary was a good mom.
MOM begins with M.
Trace and write the letter M.

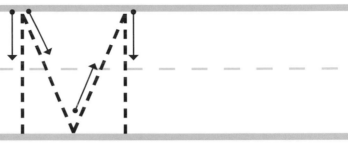

Circle the
words that
begin with M.
Use the stickers
to finish the
pictures.

Map

Boy

Jar

Moon

Marry

Men

Ark

Color in the picture of Jesus and his friend Mary.

Honor the Lord

There was another Mary in the Bible. She was a friend of Jesus. One night, Mary poured expensive perfume on Jesus' feet. Then she dried his feet with her hair. Mary understood that Jesus was very important.

Color-By-Letter

Y = Yellow   J = Purple

S = Blue   B = Brown

G = Green   M = Orange

Color in the skin tones too.

Super Girl Search

You can find the stories of many other super girls in the Bible.

Find the hidden names.

Anna	Martha
Esther	Mary
Hannah	Ruth
Lydia	Sarah

```
U  Q  S  A  R  A  H  T
G  L  Y  D  I  A  D  M
R  M  A  R  T  H  A  A
U  N  E  S  T  H  E  R
T  F  O  A  S  T  E  Y
H  A  N  N  A  H  E  I
V  I  D  N  A  Q  O  I
B  F  K  A  B  Y  R  K
```

Use the stickers to finish the pictures.

Inner Beauty

The super girls of the Bible were beautiful on the inside. Circle what is inside.

What can *you* do to become more beautiful on the inside?